RABBIT TRAVELS

by John E. McCormack

illustrated by Lynne Cherry

A UNICORN BOOK · E. P. DUTTON · NEW YORK

Text copyright © 1984 by John E. McCormack
Illustrations copyright © 1984 by Lynne Cherry

Library of Congress Cataloging in Publication Data
McCormack, John E.
   Rabbit travels.

   "A Unicorn book."
   Summary: A very fast rabbit and a very slow hare,
the best of friends, ride in a sailwagon, put up only
so long with a know-it-all frog, and build a riverboat.
   [1. Rabbits—Fiction.   2. Hares—Fiction.
3. Friendship—Fiction]   I. Cherry, Lynne, ill.
II. Title.
PZ7.M13675Rac   1984   [E]   83-14075
ISBN 0-525-44087-9

Published in the United States by E. P. Dutton, Inc.,
2 Park Avenue, New York, N.Y. 10016

·Published simultaneously in Canada by
Fitzhenry & Whiteside Limited, Toronto

Editor: Emilie McLeod   Designer: Riki Levinson

Printed in Hong Kong by South China Printing Co.
First Edition   W   10 9 8 7 6 5 4 3 2 1

to the children of long ago
Earl and Ruth,
Eleanor and Hugh

VERY FAST RABBIT
AND
VERY SLOW HARE

Once there was a very fast rabbit and a very slow hare.

Whenever they met, Hare would say, "Hello, very fast rabbit."

"Good-bye, very slow hare," Rabbit would call from a mile away.

"I HOPE YOU BROUGHT YOUR UMBRELLA," he shouted back one day. "IT IS RAINING HERE."

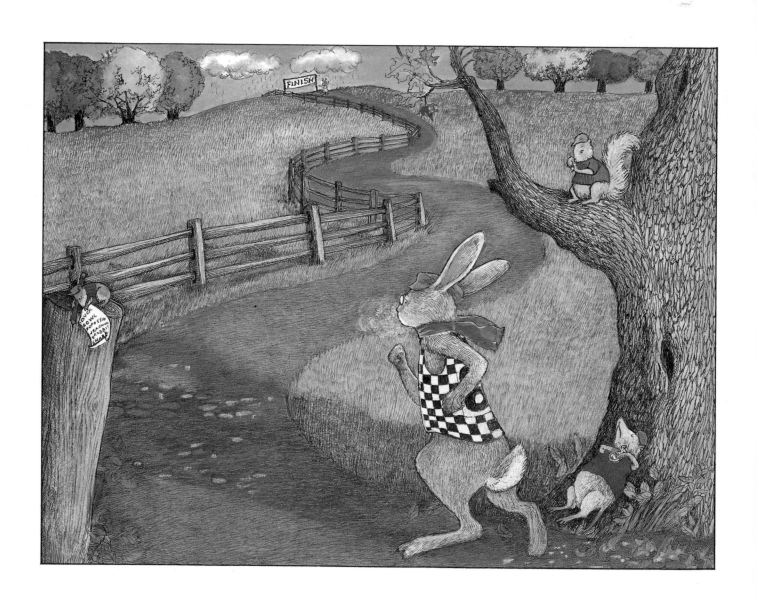

On another day, Rabbit and Hare entered a three-
legged race together.

And they won the race.

After that, Rabbit and Hare always won the three-
legged races.

And they became the best of friends, taking long,
three-legged walks together in the country.

THE SAILWAGON

One day Hare sailed into Rabbit's yard in a new wagon. "How do you like my new wagon?" he asked.

"I never saw a sailwagon before," said Rabbit. "How does it stop?"

"It has a brake," said Hare, pulling on a long, wooden handle.

"How do you steer?" asked Rabbit.

"I pull on this rope," said Hare. "Now let's go for a ride."

"OK," said Rabbit, "I'll drive."

Soon, they met Duck and Owl walking along the road,
eating ice cream.

"Come with us for a ride," shouted Rabbit.

"With pleasure," said Duck.

The wagon began to move, slowly at first, then faster.

"Here we go," cried Hare.

They sailed down a long hill.

"This is the fastest wagon in the world," cried Hare.

"My feathers!" screamed Duck.

Whoo-o-o! Whoo-o-o!

"WATCH OUT!" cried Owl. "We're driving right into a train."

"Don't worry," said Rabbit. "I'll pull on the brake."

But the wagon was going too fast to stop.

Rabbit tried to turn off the road into a field, but the rope was stuck.

Whoo-o-o! Whoo-o-o! shrieked the train.

"HELP!" cried Hare.

"SAVE ME!" shouted Owl.

"QUICK!" screamed Duck.

Rabbit was so frightened he leaped from the wagon, and the rope went with him.

Crunch! Rabbit landed in a bush.

Thud! The wagon followed.

Whoo-o-o! Whoo-o-o! The train raced past.

Rabbit felt very foolish.

Ice cream covered Hare's jacket, splattered Owl's feathers, and dribbled down Duck's vest.

"Ick!" cried Owl. "My feathers are ruined."

"Better than no feathers at all," said Duck.

"Rabbit saved us!" cried Hare. "He is a hero."

Hare had a party for Rabbit.

And when he pinned a medal on Rabbit, everyone clapped.

Tomorrow, I'll tell Hare how frightened I was, thought Rabbit as he polished his medal. But then again, maybe I won't.

THE KNOW-IT-ALL FROG

One fine day, Rabbit and Hare sailed off in a balloon with Frog.

"I hope we have fair weather," said Rabbit.

"We certainly will," said Frog. "My barometer says so, and it's always right."

As they floated over fields and forests, Frog told Rabbit
all he knew about woods and trees and farming.

"I would love to stuff a haystack in that know-it-all's
mouth," whispered Rabbit.

"It *is* his balloon," said Hare.

As they sailed over lakes and mountains, Frog told
Hare all he knew about hiking and swimming and
mountain climbing.

"I would love to tell that warty know-it-all a thing or
two," whispered Hare.

"But he already knows everything," said Rabbit.

That night, they camped out beside a small pond.

Frog told Rabbit and Hare all he knew about camping and cooking and fire tending.

Later, while Frog was asleep, Hare wrote a note and tacked it to a tree.

> Dear Frog,
>   We are hiking to the bus stop.
> Thanks for the balloon ride.
>   Hare

Then he and Rabbit left.

"I knew it," croaked Frog in the morning. "I just *knew* they would do that."

Then he sat down to breakfast all by himself.

THE HAPPY WANDERERS

On a warm summer day, Rabbit and Hare sat in the
shade of a willow tree, watching the river flow past.
  "I have an idea," said Hare. "Let's build a raft."
  "I'd rather build a clubhouse," said Rabbit.
  "A RAFT!" cried Hare.
  "A CLUBHOUSE!" shouted Rabbit.
  Rabbit stamped off upstream.
  Hare marched into the forest.

Rabbit found a large wooden box behind a supermarket.

"This box is as big as a house," he said.

Rabbit put his roller skates under the box. Then, pushing with all his strength, he rolled it down to the river.

Rabbit rushed home for his tools.

Meanwhile, Hare found some long, round logs in the forest.

"These are just what I need," he said.

Hare rolled the logs down to the river's edge.

Then he hurried home for his tools.

Rabbit sawed and hammered. He put a roof on the box. He cut out doors and windows. He put in bunk beds, a wood stove, and a bathtub.

"A wonderful job, Rabbit!" cried a voice from the river. "How do you like the raft I made?"

Rabbit was impressed. "That's no ordinary raft," he cried.

"Indeed not," said Hare proudly. "It's complete with a paddle wheel, steering wheel, pedals, and a horn." *Toot-toot!* "And it's built for speed."

Rabbit looked at the raft. Then he looked at the clubhouse.

Hare looked at the clubhouse. Then he looked at the raft.

"Are you thinking what I'm thinking?" asked Rabbit.

"Yes," said Hare. "Let's get busy."

"Now we have our very own riverboat," said Rabbit a while later.

Hare nailed a sign over the cabin door.

The sign read:

The Happy Wanderer

Rabbit and Hare moved in that day.

Then they pedaled off downstream, singing a riverboat song.

"Yo ho! Yo ho-o-o! A riverman's life for me."